Butch

Miss Loopy

poochie-poo

Poochie-Poo

Helen Stephens

David Fickling Books

OXFORD · NEW YORK

Thankyou to David (person),
Maria (person), Ness (person)
and Victor (pooch).

POOCHIE-POO
A DAVID FICKLING BOOK 0 385 60410 6

Published in Great Britain by David Fickling Books,
a division of Random House Children's Books

This edition published 2002

1 3 5 7 9 10 8 6 4 2

Copyright © Helen Stephens, 2002

The right of Helen Stephens to be identified as the author and illustrator of this work has been asserted in accordance
with the Copyright, Designs and Patents Act 1988.

Papers used by Random House Children's Books are natural, recyclable products
made from wood grown in sustainable forests. The manufacturing processes conform
to the environmental regulations of the country of origin.

Set in Bodoni MT

DAVID FICKLING BOOKS
31 Beaumont Street, Oxford, OX1 2NP
a division of RANDOM HOUSE CHILDREN'S BOOKS
61-63 Uxbridge Rd, London W5 5SA
A division of The Random House Group Ltd.

RANDOM HOUSE AUSTRALIA (PTY) LTD
20 Alfred Street, Milsons Point, Sydney,
New South Wales 2061, Australia

RANDOM HOUSE NEW ZEALAND LTD
18 Poland Road, Glenfield, Auckland 10, New Zealand

RANDOM HOUSE (PTY) LTD
Endulini, 5A Jubilee Road, Parktown 2193, South Africa

THE RANDOM HOUSE GROUP Limited Reg. No. 954009
www.randomhouse.co.uk

A CIP catalogue record for this book is available from the British Library.

Printed and bound in Singapore

Victor is a well-behaved, lovable pup and he lives with *Miss Loopy*.

Miss Loopy adores **Victor**.
She kisses him and cuddles him
whenever she can. She buys him
treats, and her favourite thing
is to tickle him under his chin
and say "Coo-chi-coo!"
Victor loves being tickled and
fussed over except . . .

. . . when his friend **Butch** comes to visit. **Butch** is a very small, very naughty pup. **Victor** thinks **Butch** is cool.

One day **Butch** came to visit. "You two pups play nicely," said *Miss Loopy*. "I'm not playing nicely," said **Butch**. "Let's play baddies." "Yes," said **Victor**. "Let's play baddies."

"Here are some doggy biscuits,
you two pups," said *Miss Loopy*.
"Delicious!" said **Victor**.

"Baddies don't eat
doggy biscuits,"
said **Butch**.
"They eat table legs!"

" Fetch my slippers, darling," said *Miss Loopy.* "Baddies don't fetch slippers," said **Butch**, "they hide them!"

"Good boy, coo-chi-coo!" said
Miss Loopy and she tickled
Victor's tummy.

"Baddies don't have their tummies
tickled," said **Butch**, "they are
too busy stealing sausages!"

"And another thing," said **Butch**, "Baddies aren't called **Victor**. They have names like Buster or Knuckles. You're a useless baddie!"

Victor felt very sad. He tried to
think of a way to show **Butch**
what a brilliant baddie he was.

No dogs allowed

Later that afternoon, when
Miss Loopy took them shopping,
Victor saw a sign that said:

"NO DOGS ALLOWED"
This gave **Victor** an idea . . .
and he told **Butch**.

"Watch this!" said **Victor**. "I'm going to run into that shop where it says "NO DOGS ALLOWED.""

Butch was very impressed.
Victor ran into the shop . . .

. . .then straight back out again! He felt terrible for being so naughty so he shouted to the shopkeeper, "Sorry about that!" "Baddies don't say sorry," said **Butch** and he laughed at **Victor** all the way home.

But **Victor** didn't care
because he didn't want
to be a baddie now.
"I wasn't cut out
for a life of crime,"
he said.

Suddenly the door bell rang. *Miss Loopy* opened the door and there stood *Miss Froopy-Frou-Frou*. "Hello, *Miss Froopy-Frou-Frou*," said *Miss Loopy*, "Come in."

"Where is my darling pup?"
cried *Miss Froopy-Frou-Frou*.
"Come to Mummikins,
my little poochie-poo.
Have you missed me?
Come on, poochie-poochie-
poochie-poo!"
And *Miss Froopy-Frou-Frou*
picked up **Butch** and
tickled his tummy.

Butch blushed.

"Baddies don't blush!" said **Victor**.

"Bye, bye," said *Miss Froopy-Frou-Frou*. "Bye, bye," called *Miss Loopy*.

"Bye, bye Poochie-poochie-poochie-poo!" said **Victor**.

Miss Froopy-Frou-Fr

Butch

Victor